What Can You Do with a Paleta?

¿Qué puedes hacer con una paleta?

by • por
CARMEN TAFOLLA

illustrated by • ilustraciones de
MAGALY MORALES

DRAGONFLY BOOKS
New York

All rights reserved. Published in the United States by Dragonfly Books,
an imprint of Random House Children's Books, a division of Random House LLC, a Penguin
Random House Company, New York. Originally published in hardcover in the United States by Tricycle Press,
an imprint of Random House Children's Books, New York, in 2009.

Dragonfly Books with the colophon is a registered trademark of Random House LLC.

Visit us on the Web! randomhouse.com/kids

Educators and librarians, for a variety of teaching tools,
visit us at RHTeachersLibrarians.com

The Library of Congress has cataloged the hardcover edition of this work as follows:
Tafolla, Carmen, 1951-
What can you do with a paleta? / by Carmen Tafolla ; illustrations by Magaly Morales.
p. cm.
Summary: A young Mexican American girl celebrates the paleta, an icy fruit popsicle,
and the many roles it plays in her lively barrio.
ISBN 978-1-58246-289-9 (trade) — ISBN 978-0-385-37452-1 (ebook)
[1. Ice pops—Fiction. 2. City and town life—Fiction. 3. Mexican Americans—Fiction.] I. Morales, Magaly, ill. II. Title.
PZ7.T1165Wh 2009 2008021051

ISBN 978-0-385-75537-5 (pbk.)

MANUFACTURED IN CHINA

17

First Dragonfly Books Edition

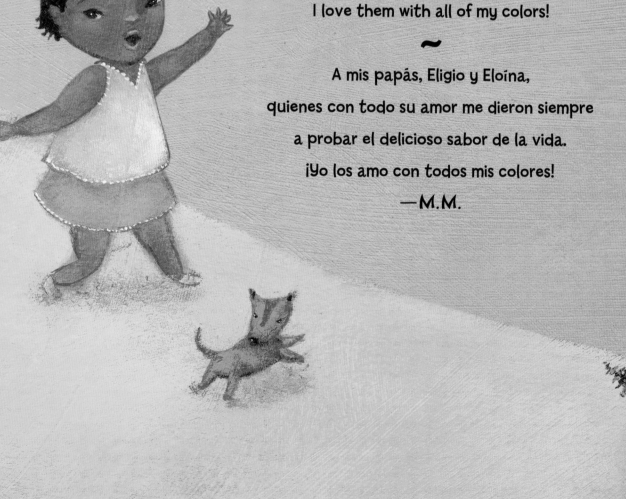

For my mother, María Duarte Tafolla,
for all the *paletas* she gave me,
and for all that she still gives my children.
~

Para mi mamá, María Duarte Tafolla,
por todas las paletas que me regaló,
y por todas las que continúa regalando a mis hijos.
—C.T.

To my parents, Eligio and Eloína,
whose infinite love is among
the most delicious flavors of life.
I love them with all of my colors!
~

A mis papás, Eligio y Eloína,
quienes con todo su amor me dieron siempre
a probar el delicioso sabor de la vida.
¡Yo los amo con todos mis colores!
—M.M.

Where the big velvet roses bloom red and pink and fuchsia,
where the accordion plays sassy and sweet,
where the smell of crispy tacos
or buttery tortillas
or juicy *fruta*
floats out of every window,

Donde las grandes rosas de terciopelo
florecen rosas, rojas y color fucsia,
donde el acordeón toca dulce y juguetón,
donde de cada ventana
sale el sabroso aroma
de tacos doraditos,
tortillas con mantequilla
o fruta jugosa,

and where the *paleta* wagon
rings its tinkly bell
and carries a treasure of icy *paletas*
in every color of the *sarape* . . .

THAT'S my *barrio!*

You can dance to the accordion,
you can smell the tacos, but . . .

y donde pasa el carrito de paletas
con su campana tintineando
y su tesoro de paletas heladas
de todos los colores del sarape . . .

¡ESE es mi barrio!

Puedes bailar al son del acordeón,
puedes oler los tacos, pero . . .

WHAT can you DO with a *paleta?*
~
¿QUÉ puedes HACER con una paleta?

You can paint your tongue purple and green,
and scare your brother!

~

Puedes pintarte la lengua de morado y verde,
¡y asustar a tu hermano!

Or maybe learn to make tough decisions.
Strawberry? Or coconut?

~

O quizá aprender a tomar decisiones difíciles.
¿Fresa? ¿O coco?

You can make new friends,

~

Puedes hacer nuevos amigos,

give yourself a big, blue mustache,
~
pintarte un bigote gigante y azul,

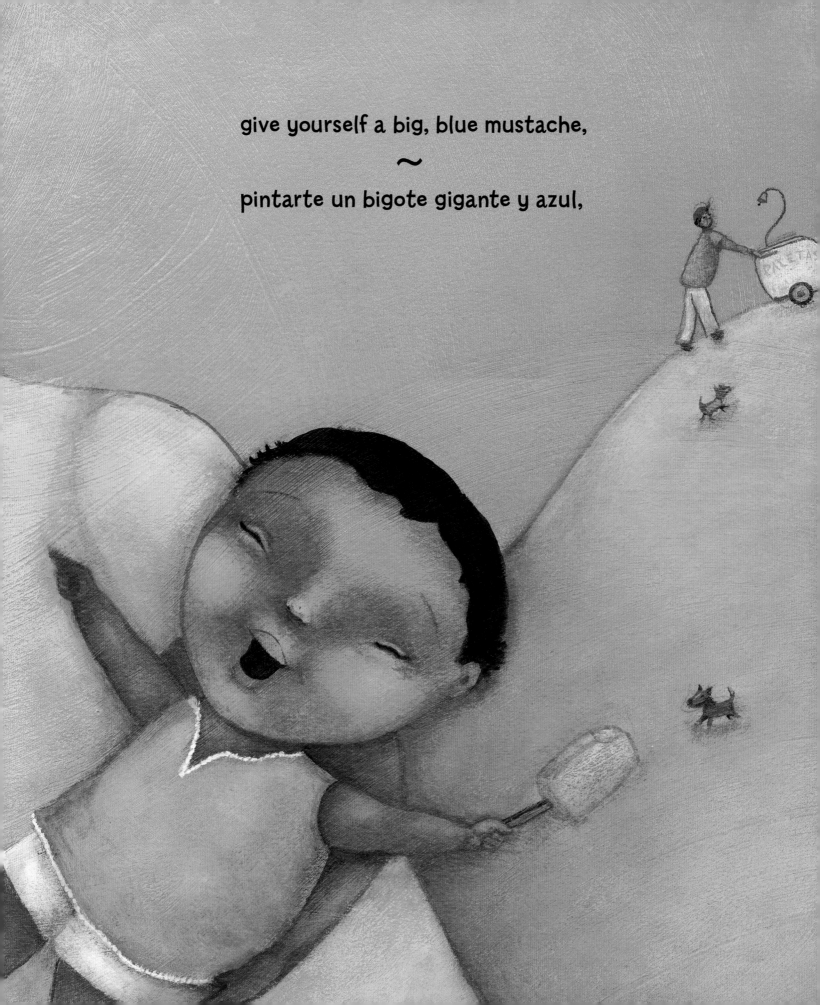

or create a masterpiece!

~

¡o crear una obra maestra!

You can use one to cool off, like Mama does!

~

Puedes usar una paleta para refrescarte,
¡como lo hace Mamá!

Tío once won a baseball game
by offering one to the batter
(right when the ball was being pitched!).

~

Una vez Tío ganó un juego de béisbol
por darle una paleta al bateador
(¡justo en el momento en que le lanzaban la pelota!).

You can help the *señora* at the fruit stand
make it through a long, hard day.

~

Puedes ayudar a la señora de la frutería
a sentir el día menos largo.

But I think the very best thing
to do with a *paleta* is to . . .

lick it and slurp it
and sip it and munch it
and gobble it all down.

Where the big, velvet roses
bloom red and pink and fuchsia,

~

Pero creo que lo mejor
que puedes hacer con una paleta es . . .

chuparla y morderla
y lamerla y tragarla
y beberla en gotitas.

Donde las grandes rosas de terciopelo
florecen rosas, rojas y color fucsia,

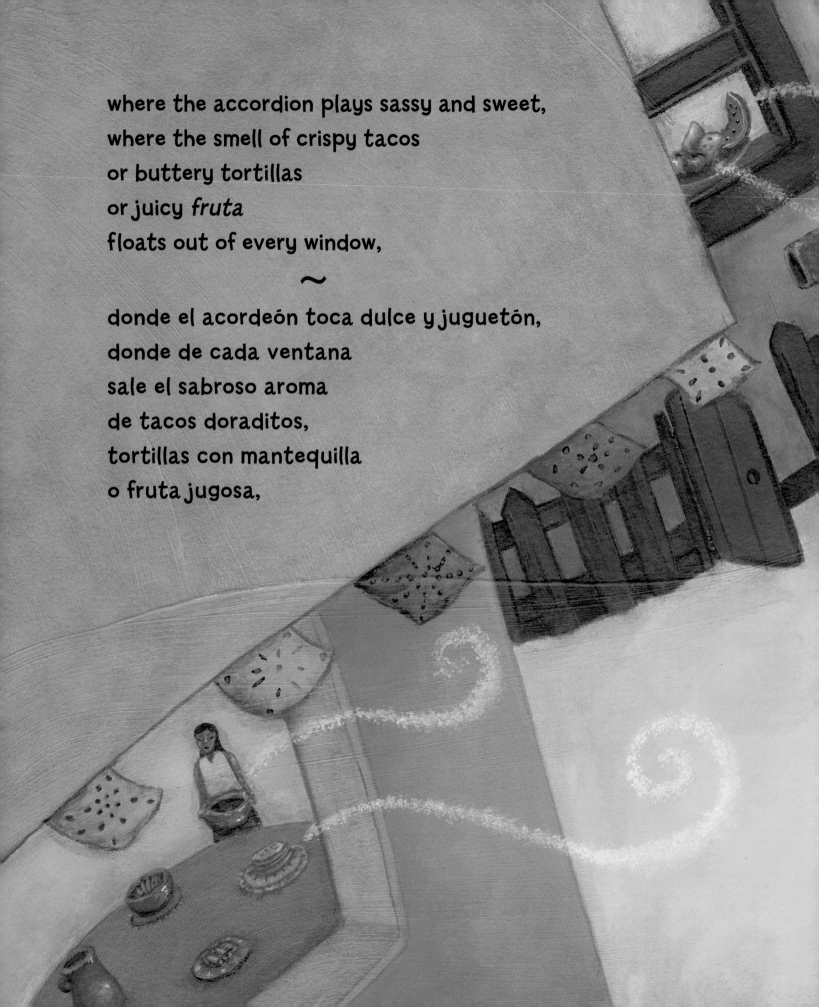

where the accordion plays sassy and sweet,
where the smell of crispy tacos
or buttery tortillas
or juicy *fruta*
floats out of every window,

~

donde el acordeón toca dulce y juguetón,
donde de cada ventana
sale el sabroso aroma
de tacos doraditos,
tortillas con mantequilla
o fruta jugosa,

and where the *paleta* wagon
rings its tinkly bell
and carries a treasure of icy *paletas*
in every color of the *sarape*...

THAT'S my *barrio!*

~

y donde pasa el carrito de paletas
con su campana tintineando
y su tesoro de paletas heladas
de todos los colores del sarape...

¡ESE es mi barrio!

ABOUT *PALETAS*

A much-anticipated event in any Latino *barrio* ("neighborhood") is the arrival of the *paleta* wagon. The *paleta* man comes pushing his cart down the street, tinkling a bell and shouting, "*Pale-ta-a-a-as!*" for everyone to hear. The wagon carries sweet, juicy, ice-cold *paletas* made from all-natural, healthy ingredients.

Paletas come in many delicious flavors. Here are some of them below.
Which is YOUR favorite?

~

ACERCA DE LAS PALETAS

Un evento siempre esperado en cualquier barrio mexicano o latino es la llegada del paletero. El paletero viene empujando su carrito por la calle, tintineando una campanita y gritando "¡Pale-ta-a-a-as!" para que todos lo escuchen. El carrito trae paletas heladas, jugosas, y dulces, hechas de ingredientes naturales y saludables.

Las paletas vienen en muchos sabores deliciosos. Aqui hay algunos.
¿Cual es TU favorito?

Watermelon / Sandía

Berry / Mora

Mango / Mango

Pecan / Nuez

Coconut / Coco

Strawberry / Fresa

Grape / Uva

Lime / Limón

Banana / Plátano

Hibiscus / Jamaica